DC SUPER HERO FAIRY TALES

AQUAMAN AND THE RAPUNZEL PLOT

by Laurie S. Sutton
illustrated by Agnes Garbowska
colors by Sil Brys

STONE ARCH BOOKS
a capstone imprint

Published by Stone Arch Books, an imprint of Capstone
1710 Roe Crest Drive, North Mankato, Minnesota 56003
capstonepub.com

Library of Congress Cataloging-in-Publication Data
Names: Sutton, Laurie, author. | Garbowska, Agnes, illustrator. |
Brys, Silvana, colorist.
Title: Aquaman and the Rapunzel plot / by Laurie S. Sutton ; illustrated
by Agnes Garbowska ; colors by Sil Brys.
Description: North Mankato, Minnesota : Stone Arch Books, [2022] |
Series: DC super hero fairy tales | Audience: Ages 8–11 | Audience:
Grades 4–6 | Summary: "Aquaman's underwater kingdom is facing a
medical threat. Luckily, a sea witch offers him a rare plant to fight the
sickness . . . in exchange for a hefty price. But the Sea King soon discovers
she isn't just greedy. The old woman has locked the true owner of the crop in
an enchanted coral tower! What's worse, the trapped mermaid thinks she's
being protected not imprisoned, so her living seaweed hair is ready to fight
off any stranger who climbs inside. Can the Atlantean hero partner with the
coral captive to end the witch's fishy scheme? In this twisted retelling,
DC Super Heroes and Super-Villains collide with the Rapunzel fairy tale to
create an action-packed chapter book for kids!"— Provided by publisher.
Identifiers: LCCN 2021029896 (print) | LCCN 2021029897 (ebook) | ISBN
9781663959072 (hardcover) | ISBN 9781666328967 (paperback) | ISBN
9781666328974 (pdf)
Subjects: CYAC: Fairy tales. | Superheroes—Fiction. | Characters in
literature—Fiction. | LCGFT: Superhero fiction. | Fairy tales.
Classification: LCC PZ8.S92 Aq 2022 (print) | LCC PZ8.S92 (ebook) |
DDC [Fic]—dc23
LC record available at https://lccn.loc.gov/2021029896
LC ebook record available at https://lccn.loc.gov/2021029897

Designed by Hilary Wacholz

Printed and bound in the USA. PO4608

TABLE OF CONTENTS

ONCE UPON A TIME ...

THE WORLD'S GREATEST
SUPER HEROES COLLIDED WITH
THE WORLD'S BEST-KNOWN
FAIRY TALES TO CREATE ...

DC SUPER HERO
FAIRY TALES

Now, Aquaman has discovered
something fishy in an old sea
witch's garden, where gold
seaweed strands stream down
from a tall coral tower. It's up
to the hero to investigate in this
twisted retelling of "Rapunzel"!

CHAPTER 1

NEPTUNE'S FIN

Aquaman, King of the Seven Seas, rode on the back of a large seahorse named Storm through deep, unfamiliar waters.

WOOOSH!

Beside them, a giant squid slowly surged forward. The creature was an old lord of the deep known only as Ancient Elder. He was guiding Aquaman through the dark. He was tremendous in size, but he swam at the pace of a sea snail.

Are we almost there, Ancient Elder?
Aquaman asked, using his telepathy
to talk to the sea beast.

Humans . . . are always . . . in a hurry,
the squid replied slowly.

*True, but sometimes there is a good reason
for it,* Aquaman said. *Atlantis is in desperate
need. My people are sick. I need to get the cure
to them as soon as possible.*

Over the last few days, an illness had
been spreading through the underwater
city of Atlantis. Ancient Elder had told
Aquaman about a sea plant that could
make a powerful medicine to fight it.
The plant, Neptune's Fin, was very rare.

But Ancient Elder had seen places
in the ocean that the Sea King had not.
He knew where to find the plant.

The gigantic squid led the hero into the depths. The water was as dark as night. Aquaman wondered what kind of plant could live this far from the reach of sunlight.

Not far . . . now, the old squid said.

Aquaman saw a faint glow in the distance. As they came closer, he realized the light was coming from a dome of shimmering algae. At its base was a huge circular wall made of dark coral. A tall tower rose up within.

The plant . . . grows inside, Ancient Elder said. *Beware . . . the witch.*

Wait. What witch? Aquaman asked. But the squid was already swimming away.

The Sea King faced the dome. The coral base was as sharp as thorns. The glowing algae cast a ghostly light.

I'll just have to be on my guard, Aquaman thought. *I will risk dealing with a sea witch to save the people of Atlantis.*

Aquaman rode Storm around the wall till he came to an archway. It held a door made of spiral narwhal tusks. The door was closed.

Aquaman slid off Storm's back and swam over. He raised his hand to knock, but the door suddenly opened.

FWOOOSH!

An old merwoman floated before the Sea King. Her shark tail churned the water. Pale white hair swirled around her head.

"Who are you?" the merwoman asked sharply.

"I'm Aquaman, King of Atlantis," Aquaman replied. "And who are you?"

"I am Gothal. This is my home," the merwoman said. "What are you doing here? No one has come here for years."

"My people are ill, and I've come for the sea plant that will help cure them," Aquaman explained. "I was told that it grows here."

"*Ahhh*. You want Neptune's Fin. Well, the plant isn't free, King Aquaman!" Gothal said. She eyed Storm and then declared, "I want that seahorse as payment! I'm getting too old to swim on my own."

"I need Storm," Aquaman said. "But I can come back later with a different seahorse."

The merwoman narrowed her black eyes as she considered the bargain. "The seahorse must have a gold saddle and a bridle with jewels," she said. "And you must give me Storm's gold saddle now as a down payment."

"Deal," Aquaman replied. "I will make sure you ride in style."

"Then you may come into my garden," Gothal said. "But be quick about it."

Aquaman followed Gothal into the dome. It was much brighter inside. Tall stalks of kelp and blooming sea flowers filled the space. Tiny, colorful fish swam among the plants like honeybees.

"This garden is beautiful, Gothal," Aquaman said. "How do you take care of it all by yourself?"

The old merwoman shrugged and replied, "I manage."

"You said it was getting hard to swim on your own. I could bring people to help you when I return," Aquaman offered.

"No!" Gothal said. "I like my privacy."

Aquaman said nothing more. *Gothal has to be the sea witch Ancient Elder warned me about,* he thought. *She doesn't seem dangerous. Just cranky. Although, it is odd to live in such a dark, faraway place all alone.*

The hero glanced at the dark coral tower in the garden's center. It was out of place in all the bright beauty.

"Nothing to see there!" Gothal snapped.

She hurried Aquaman to a patch of sea plants growing in huge clumps. The leaves were a vivid green. Small violet flowers grew up from the middle on thin stems.

"Neptune's Fin," Gothal said with a wide gesture. "Cut only the leaves. Do not take the roots or flowers."

The merwoman watched Aquaman closely as he took a sack from behind Storm's saddle. Then he began picking leaves.

PLUCK! PLUCK! PLUCK!

It did not take Aquaman long to fill the bag. He tied it onto Storm's back and removed the seahorse's golden saddle.

Gothal snatched her payment. She quickly led the hero and his steed out the garden gate.

"You have what you need, King. Now go. But don't forget the rest of my payment," she reminded Aquaman.

Before he could reply, the old merwoman slammed the door closed.

Gothal could not wait for me to leave! Aquaman thought as he leaped onto Storm's back. *Maybe she does just like her privacy . . . or she's hiding something.*

The Sea King had not gone far when he heard an unusual sound. It drifted through the water like a gentle current. It took him a moment to realize it was a song. It was beautiful. It filled his whole body with joy.

Even Storm was affected. The seahorse slowly came to a stop to listen.

Is that Gothal singing? Aquaman thought, captivated.

Even though it was urgent to get back to Atlantis, Aquaman couldn't resist. He turned Storm around. He headed back to the sea garden. When he reached the algae dome, he pushed through the slimy wall to peek inside.

Gothal floated at the base of the coral tower. But she wasn't singing. Instead, she called out, "Rarazel, Rarazel! Let down your golden fronds!"

The singing stopped. A cascade of gold seaweed tumbled down from a lone window high up on the tower. Gothal gripped the fronds and was lifted up into the building.

What were those seaweed tendrils? Aquaman wondered. *And who or what is Rarazel? It seems Gothal really is hiding something out here.*

Storm shifted under the hero, as if anxious to be on their way.

I'll investigate when I return, Aquaman thought. *But right now, I must deliver the Neptune's Fin to Atlantis.*

The Sea King urged Storm to top speed. They rode off into the dark waters toward home.

WOOOOSH!

CHAPTER 2

FRIEND OR FOE?

Aquaman returned to the undersea garden a week later. He brought with him a beautiful seahorse and the thanks of a grateful kingdom. Using the Neptune's Fin, the Atlantean doctors had created a cure for the illness affecting the city. Now, Aquaman was back to make good on his promise.

The Sea King opened the dome's door and called for Gothal. When she did not come, Aquaman entered the garden. He led the seahorse to the base of the coral tower.

"Gothal!" Aquaman called to the single window. "Gothal! I have brought your seahorse!"

There was still no answer. The hero started to worry that the old merwoman was injured or ill inside the tower.

What if Gothal caught the same sickness that swept through my kingdom? Aquaman wondered. *Oh no. What if I accidentally brought it here from Atlantis?*

Concerned, Aquaman started to swim up to the window. He had gone only a few feet when—

WHUUUMP!

The water was clear, but Aquaman felt like he had hit an invisible wall. He sank back to the ocean floor in surprise.

That's strange, he thought.

He tried to climb up the spiky coral wall instead of swimming, but—

WHUUUUMP!

There's some sort of unseen barrier blocking me from reaching the window! Aquaman realized. *Gothal must have a magic spell to protect the tower. I guess it's her "home security system." But if she's in trouble, how can I get up there to help?*

Then Aquaman remembered seeing Gothal getting pulled up by seaweed. She had said a specific phrase to summon it.

Aquaman repeated the phrase. "Rarazel! Rarazel! Let down your golden fronds!"

A moment later, thick strands of beautiful golden seaweed appeared. They flowed down from the window.

SWOOOOSH!

As soon as Aquaman grasped the silky fronds, they started drawing him up.

The seaweed fronds have no trouble moving through the water, Aquaman thought.

Soon, the gold fronds had brought him to the arched window. He let go and stepped inside the tower.

The fronds continued to withdraw across a large room. Algae glowed on the smooth coral walls. Sea flowers grew up from dozens of containers in all shapes and sizes that were scattered around the room. It was like a miniature garden inside the tower. There was barely space for a few pieces of furniture. They looked as if they had been made from old shipwreck scraps.

"Gothal? Are you all right?" Aquaman called.

As he swam farther inside, he did not find the old merwoman. Instead, Aquaman discovered a beautiful mermaid! Her back was turned to him as she sat on what looked like a giant, squishy jellyfish. Her tail and fins sparkled with gold scales and amber patches.

But the mermaid's hair was unlike anything Aquaman had ever seen. It was the very same gold fronds that had lifted him into the tower. He watched in awe as the seaweed strands drifted the rest of the way across the room and shrank back into her scalp.

"Back so soon, Gothal?" the mermaid asked. She was reading a seaweed scroll and did not look up.

"I'm not Gothal. My name is Aquaman," the Sea King replied. "Hello."

The mermaid whipped around. Her eyes widened in fear and alarm as she saw the Super Hero for the first time.

Then her hair fronds shot out from her head. They swirled around her like a halo of sea snakes. The mermaid looked like an underwater Medusa.

"I'm sorry! I didn't mean to barge in on you!" Aquaman said.

Suddenly the edges of the fronds became hard and sharp. They surged toward Aquaman.

The Sea King grasped a couple of the tendrils in his fists. The rest wrapped around his legs and chest. He twisted to keep from being completely tangled up.

"Stop! Please! I won't hurt you!" Aquaman called.

The mermaid's only reply was to toss her head and swing Aquaman around the room. He slammed into the walls, the floor, and the potted sea plants.

WHOOOMP! THWUUUMP! CRAAASH!

The mermaid did not seem to care about the wreckage. Aquaman gritted his teeth, but his sea-hardened body was not harmed by the blows.

The Sea King pushed off from one of the walls and sped like a torpedo toward the mermaid. Gripping the ends of the fronds, he swam around and around her at amazing speed. Soon, she was wrapped up in her own golden hair.

"I promise I'm not going to hurt you," Aquaman said.

THWAAAAP!

The mermaid struck Aquaman with her powerful tail. The hit jarred his hands loose from her fronds. He was tossed onto the jellyfish couch on the far side of the room.

WHOOOOMP!

Free from Aquaman's grip, the mermaid unwrapped herself from the tangled tendrils. They fanned out like angry octopus tentacles as she pressed her back against the wall.

"Go away, monster! Leave me alone!" the mermaid shouted.

She's terrified of me, Aquaman thought. *I don't think she's ever seen someone who isn't a mer-person! How do I make her feel safe?*

He held up his hands. "Please, no more fighting."

The Sea King did not move on the jellyfish couch. He did not even look at the mermaid.

Gothal never said anyone else was living in her home! Aquaman thought. *It seems she has a few secrets hidden in her garden.*

"Who . . . who are you?" the mermaid asked at last. Her voice was soft and musical.

"My name is Arthur Curry, but most people call me Aquaman," the Sea King replied. He looked up at her. "What's your name?"

"I'm Rarazel," the mermaid said. Her hair fronds started to relax.

"That's a beautiful name," Aquaman said. "I'm sorry that I frightened you."

"Where's your tail?" Rarazel asked.

"I don't have one. I'm not a mer-person," Aquaman replied.

The mermaid looked alarmed again. Her hair thrashed.

"You *are* a monster!" Rarazel gasped. "Gothal says there are dangerous monsters beyond the tower!"

"I'm not a monster," Aquaman assured her. He did not move a muscle. "And I promise that I'm not dangerous. I'm the King of Atlantis and a Super Hero. Honest."

"King . . . Arthur?" Rarazel asked. Her hair fronds floated gently again as she calmed down.

"Just call me Aquaman," the Sea King said. He smiled at the uncertain mermaid. "Have you never been outside this tower?"

"No! It's too scary!" Rarazel said with a shiver. "Gothal says so over and over. That is why she brought me here as a little child. She used her magic to grow the coral around me to protect me."

"And . . . you've had no visitors in all that time?" Aquaman asked.

"No. You're the first one," Rarazel replied.

"I suppose that makes sense, since the only way in here is to be pulled up by your hair fronds," Aquaman said. "It really limits your social life."

"That was Gothal's magic," Rarazel said with a shrug. "I don't know how it works. All I know is that it keeps me safe from danger."

Something is wrong here, Aquaman thought. *There are easier ways to protect a child than growing an entire coral tower and casting a tricky spell. Even after all that, why make Rarazel so afraid of what's outside the tower? What is Gothal up to?*

CHAPTER 3

A MATTER OF TRUST

Aquaman was starting to suspect there was more to the old sea witch. *But how does Rarazel play into everything?* he wondered.

"Where is Gothal now?" Aquaman asked.

"She went to deliver a harvest from the garden," Rarazel said.

"She tells you to be afraid of what's outside the tower, but she isn't," Aquaman noted.

"Gothal has magic to protect her," Rarazel replied.

"Your fronds are pretty powerful too," Aquaman said. He looked around at the plants and furniture that had fallen over during their struggle. "Let me help you clean up the mess we made."

Aquaman began to straighten up the room. The mermaid soon joined him. He was glad that she was starting to feel comfortable around him.

After a while, the hero found what looked like a giant treasure chest. It had tipped onto its side. Coins, gems, jewelry, and other precious items had spilled out onto the floor.

"That's what I'd call a king's ransom!" Aquaman said.

"Oh no! That's Gothal's chest! She said to never open it!" Rarazel cried. Her hair fronds started to swirl.

"It was an accident," Aquaman said, trying to calm her. "I can put it all back."

The hero used his sea-strengthened muscles to lift the huge chest upright. He began picking up strands of giant pearls and silver bracelets covered with gems. He gathered the loose treasures one by one. Then he dropped them into the chest and slammed the lid.

THWUUUMP!

"See? All gone," Aquaman said. Then a thought occurred to him. "Why would Gothal forbid you to see what's inside the chest?"

"I don't know. It's Gothal's chest," Rarazel replied nervously.

"Well, she sure likes precious things," Aquaman said. "No wonder she asked for a seahorse, a jeweled bridle, and two gold saddles as payment for Neptune's Fin."

"Payment? No. Neptune's Fin is given freely to all in need," Rarazel replied. "So are all the garden plants. I sing to them, and they grow. I love making the garden so lush and full."

Aquaman was silent for a moment. *So Rarazel is doing all the work of growing the plants,* he realized. *But she doesn't know Gothal is secretly selling them for profit! How do I break it to her?*

"So that was *you* singing," Aquaman began. "It was beautiful. I would have come back to find out who it was even if I didn't have to return with Gothal's payment."

"Neptune's Fin is free," Rarazel repeated. "Gothal said so!"

Aquaman swam to the window and pointed outside. "Yet she demanded *that.*"

Rarazel glided over. She saw the bejeweled seahorse waiting in the garden.

"And I think the treasure chest proves that I'm not the only one who has had to pay," Aquaman said gently. "I am sorry to say this . . . but Gothal might not have been truthful."

The Sea King could see Rarazel starting to get upset with that possibility. Her golden hair fronds swirled.

She's trusted Gothal all her life, Aquaman thought. *This could be a huge betrayal. Maybe a little distraction can help comfort her for now.*

"Rarazel, would you like to see the seahorse dance? Look!" Aquaman said.

He sent out a telepathic command. Below, the seahorse began to spin around stalks of flowering kelp.

Rarazel let out a small, melodic laugh. "Oh! That's pretty!"

"Would you like to pet him?" Aquaman asked.

"But outside . . . it's dangerous," Rarazel said. "I—I've never gone out of the tower."

"We can stay in the garden. I will give you a ride on the seahorse through the plants," the Sea King said. He bowed dramatically. "You'll be like a princess touring her realm."

"What's a princess?" Rarazel asked.

"There are so many things for you to learn," Aquaman said with a smile. "First, let's get you out of this tower."

The Super Hero held out his hand. The mermaid started to take it, but then she pulled back.

"I can't. Gothal's spell stops anyone from entering or leaving the tower unless I lift or lower them with my fronds," Rarazel said. "I can't climb down my own hair."

Aquaman thought for a moment. He swam to the heavy treasure chest. He lifted it with his sea-strength and brought it over.

"Here. Wrap a couple of your fronds around the chest," Aquaman said.

Rarazel looked unsure. But she grabbed the chest with a few seaweed strands.

"Now, you can let out those fronds, and the chest will anchor them while you lower yourself out the window," Aquaman said. "I'll use them to climb down right beside you."

The fronds grew longer, and Rarazel leaned backward into the window opening. Suddenly she stopped.

"I . . . I can't go through the window," Rarazel said.

"Don't be afraid. I will be with you and will keep you safe," Aquaman said.

"No. I mean that I can't pass through Gothal's spell," Rarazel said. "I can't leave the tower even though I'm using my hair. Even though I want to."

The mermaid relaxed her fronds and let go of the treasure chest. She looked confused and disappointed as she floated back into the tower room.

"I don't understand," she said.

"I do," Aquaman replied with a frown.

It was all making sense now. The sea witch's plot was even worse than he had first thought.

"Gothal's magic not only keeps people out. It keeps *you* in. You're a prisoner," he explained. "She won't let you go because you grow the Neptune's Fin and she reaps the benefit. This has been her scheme all along."

"Gothal . . . has *used* me," Rarazel whispered, finally realizing the truth. Her fronds started to twist. "I trusted her all this time."

"Don't worry," Aquaman promised. "I will help you leave this tower. If that's what you want."

Rarazel locked eyes with the hero. "Yes," she said. "I trust you."

CHAPTER 4

THE TRUTH REVEALED

"We have to find a way to get you out of the tower," Aquaman said to Rarazel.

He looked down at the colorful garden below as he tried to think of an answer. He watched the honeybee fish swim busily around the blossoms.

"Gothal's spell keeps *people* out. Maybe it doesn't affect sea animals!" he realized.

The Sea King used his telepathy to tell the fish to swim to the window. They did so easily.

"It looks like I'm right!" Aquaman said. "This gives me an idea. I'll summon some of my largest sea-subjects. They can break down the room's walls. The spell can't keep you from leaving a window that no longer exists. You will be free!"

He sent out a telepathic call for help. In the garden, the seahorse rushed toward the coral tower, but no other creatures came.

"*Hmm.* I'm not getting a reply from anyone outside the dome," Aquaman said. "Gothal's magic must be limiting the range of my telepathy. I have to go beyond the garden and find where her magic ends."

"Promise me that you'll come back," Rarazel said.

"I promise," Aquaman replied. "I give you my word as Sea King."

Rarazel let her golden fronds out the window. Aquaman grasped the ends as the strands flowed down the side of the tower. The honeybee fish followed alongside him. He was greeted by the seahorse when he reached the ground.

Thank you for coming at my call, the Sea King told them. *But I'm going to need some larger friends.*

Aquaman swam to the garden gate. The seahorse and little fish followed him like enthusiastic puppies.

Stay! Aquaman ordered them. *Look after Rarazel while I'm gone. I'll be back soon.*

The seahorse snorted a stream of bubbles and nodded its head. The honeybee fish stood at attention like soldiers. Aquaman smiled at his loyal sea-subjects.

He turned to wave goodbye to Rarazel.
Then he swam out of the narwhal-tusk gate
and into the darkness.

Aquaman sped through the water. He sent
out bursts of telepathy every few moments
like sonar. No one replied.

*How can Gothal's magic be so strong to block
my telepathy?* Aquaman thought. *It seems I've
underestimated her.*

I warned you . . . about . . . the witch,
a familiar voice finally replied.

Ancient Elder! Aquaman said.

The shadowy mass of the giant squid
came into view. The Sea King floated close
to one of the creature's enormous eyes.

Thank you for answering my telepathic call,
Aquaman said.

I was . . . nearby, Ancient Elder replied.

You were right about the witch, Aquaman said. *But why didn't you tell me that she's holding a mermaid prisoner in the tower?*

Rarazel, Ancient Elder said. *She lives . . . in the tower. Not . . . a prisoner.*

Gothal's magic traps Rarazel inside. She can't get out, Aquaman said.

I did not . . . know that, the squid replied.

Well, now Rarazel wants to leave, Aquaman said. *I need to summon some friends to help her do that, but my telepathy is blocked.*

The zone . . . of silence . . . goes far, Ancient Elder explained. *It ends where . . . the water turns . . . from dark to light . . . from cold to cool.*

Thank you, Ancient Elder, Aquaman said.

The Sea King started to swim upward, but the old squid reached out and grasped one of his ankles. Aquaman paused.

I want . . . to help . . . Rarazel, Ancient Elder said. *I enjoy . . . her songs.*

And you shall help, Aquaman replied. *Wait here. I plan to have some very large finny friends with me when I return. You'll fit right in.*

❦ ❧

When Gothal came back to the garden, she was carrying a small bag of treasure. It was payment for a harvest of Neptune's Fin.

She soon saw another payment waiting for her. The seahorse with the jeweled bridle and gold saddle floated near the coral tower. She did not see Aquaman.

He must have brought the seahorse and left, Gothal thought. *Good. I don't need him finding out about Rarazel. I can't grow Neptune's Fin without her. She's a secret that I don't want to share.*

The merwoman swam to the seahorse to admire the beautiful bridle, but the creature shied away. It snorted out bubbles. Suddenly honeybee fish swarmed around her.

"What has gotten into you?" Gothal said, swatting at the fish. "Go away!"

Gothal pushed past them to the base of the tower. She called out, and soon seaweed fronds pulled her up. She was very surprised to see that much of the tower room was wrecked.

"Rarazel! What happened here?" Gothal gasped.

"I was surprised by a visitor," Rarazel replied.

"Aquaman!" Gothal said. Then she muttered, "That nosy Sea King! Why couldn't he just drop off my seahorse and leave?"

Rarazel's hair fronds started to swirl. "So, what Aquaman said was true. The seahorse *was* payment. You are demanding treasures in exchange for Neptune's Fin."

"Of course not. Aquaman was lying," Gothal replied. She hid the little bag behind her back.

"I don't think so. I . . . I saw what was in the chest," Rarazel admitted.

"*What?!*" Gothal shouted angrily. She swam to the treasure chest and opened the lid. Then she looked relieved. "Good. Nothing is missing."

"All that's payment, isn't it?" Rarazel asked. "Neptune's Fin is supposed to be free!"

Gothal said nothing at first. Then she let out a sigh and emptied her bag into the treasure chest. "Yes. Fine. I lied. It's payment," she replied.

"And you lied about the tower keeping me safe! It's really a prison," Rarazel said.

"Yes. I lied about that too," Gothal said. She turned toward Rarazel. "I lied about everything. What are you going to do about it?"

Hurt and anger churned inside Rarazel. Gothal's betrayal overwhelmed her. The mermaid's golden fronds struck out at the sea witch.

Gothal struck back.

CHAPTER 5

Fight for Freedom

ZAAAAP!

The sea witch shot a bolt of energy from her hands like an electric eel. It pushed Rarazel across the room and into the wall.

THWUUUMP!

"Silly child," Gothal said. "You can't defeat me. You'll stay in this tower and grow Neptune's Fin for me for the rest of your life. I will become richer than your precious Sea King!"

"No," Rarazel said as she got back up. "Aquaman will free me."

"Not if I destroy him first," Gothal replied.

The mermaid's hair fronds writhed as if they had a life of their own. "Leave him alone!" she shouted.

Rarazel's golden fronds turned stiff and sharp. They zoomed toward the sea witch. The fronds moved so fast that they wrapped around Gothal before she could react.

SWOOOOSH! SWOOOOSH!

Rarazel tossed her head and knocked the sea witch against the wall. She whipped her head again. Gothal smacked into the treasure chest. The lid flew open, and the sparkling contents scattered across the room.

"*Uuuuh.* You'll pay for that!" Gothal said. Her body crackled with electrical energy.

ZZZAAAAP!

The energy raced up Rarazel's fronds. The mermaid shuddered, and then she floated slowly to the floor. The shock had knocked her out.

Gothal struggled to pull free from the seaweed fronds wrapped around her. But a few moments later, the fronds fell away by themselves.

They're dead, she realized. *But I need them! I can't leave the tower without them!*

The sea witch looked over to where Rarazel rested on the floor. All her gold fronds were now black and shriveled.

Oh no. I'm trapped in here by my own spell! Gothal thought.

Aquaman raced toward the glowing algae dome. A huge sperm whale and two massive orcas followed closely behind. Ancient Elder swam as swiftly as his old tentacles allowed.

Get ready, Rarazel! Aquaman called with his telepathy. *Things are about to get bumpy!*

The Sea King and his giant sea-subjects burst through the gooey algae dome. Moments later, the whale swam right up to the coral tower. The protective spell didn't slow the sea creature.

The whale rammed its blunt head into the top of the structure.

THOOOOM!

The orcas attacked the sides.

THWAAAAM! THWAAAAM!

The coral started to crack.

It's working! Aquaman told his sea-subjects. *Keep hammering!*

THOOOM! THWAAAM!

Ancient Elder wrapped his powerful tentacles around the top of the weakened tower.

RIIIIP!

The whole roof was torn away.

Rarazel's room was now exposed to open water. Aquaman easily zoomed inside.

"See, Rarazel?" he called. "I told you I would come back with my finny friends."

The Sea King was shocked to find the mermaid lying on the floor surrounded by black fronds. He sped over to her. The fronds fell from Rarazel's head as he lifted her into his arms.

"This is all your fault, Sea King!" Gothal shrieked as she swam out from behind a pile of broken coral. She started to gather her scattered jewels. "You've ruined everything!"

"No, it's your own greed that has ruined everything," Aquaman said. He set Rarazel down and turned to face the sea witch. The whale, orcas, and old squid crowded behind the Sea King to back him up. "Your scamming days are over, Gothal."

Furious, the sea witch let out a screech and one final blast of magical energy at the Super Hero.

ZZZZZAAAAP!

The dazzling light hit Aquaman with the force of a charging hammerhead shark. It sent him flying backward out of the wrecked tower.

But a giant tentacle caught the Sea King.

I . . . have you, Ancient Elder said as he gently put Aquaman on the ground.

With another tentacle, the giant squid grabbed Gothal. She did not struggle. She had no more magic or strength left to resist.

"Ancient Elder, what's going on? Where's Rarazel?" Aquaman asked, rubbing his eyes. "The light blast made it hard to see."

She . . . is here, the old squid said.

He used a tentacle to lower the mermaid into the hero's arms. The honeybee fish circled anxiously. The orcas and whale hovered overhead. The seahorse gently nudged her.

Rarazel opened her eyes. She looked at Aquaman, then at Gothal wrapped up in the giant squid's tentacle. She gasped when she finally saw the broken coral tower.

"W-what happened?" Rarazel asked.

"I came back with my sea-subjects and broke through the tower like I promised," Aquaman replied. "But what happened to *you*?"

"Gothal . . . came back. We fought," Rarazel said softly. Then she touched her head. "My . . . fronds. Take me . . . to Neptune's Fin."

The crowd of sea-subjects guided the mermaid and half-blind hero through the garden to a patch of Neptune's Fin. Rarazel sang weakly as she pulled a plant from the ground, roots and all. The mermaid nibbled on the flowers, leaves, and the carrot-like root. Her song grew stronger with every bite. Soon new fronds began to bud all over her head.

"Eat this," Rarazel said as she handed Aquaman a root. "It will speed up your recovery too."

Aquaman munched on the plant. "Gothal didn't let me harvest the root."

"I should have and then made you pay extra for it," the sea witch muttered.

"It's the most powerful part," Rarazel explained. "It's called Neptune's Tail."

"Ah, it's working. My eyesight is clearing!" Aquaman said.

"I'm glad," Rarazel said. She looked up at the ruined tower. "It makes me sad that my home is destroyed. But I'm also happy because now I am free. Still, I don't know what to do with that freedom."

"I have some ideas," Aquaman said.

A few days later, Aquaman swam through a lush garden near his royal palace in Atlantis. He passed by kelp flowers and colorful plants. Then, amid of huge cluster of Neptune's Fin, he found Rarazel. Honeybee fish buzzed around her as she tended to new seedlings.

"How do you like your new home, Rarazel?" Aquaman asked.

The mermaid rushed over, swimming in circles around the Sea King. Her long, gold fronds had grown back, and they trailed behind her.

"I love it! Thank you for moving all my plants here. There's so much space and light!" Rarazel replied. "And all the people I've met are so kind. Gothal lied about there being monsters beyond the garden."

"Gothal can't hurt you or tell anymore lies now that she's in an Atlantean jail," Aquaman said.

"Yes. It's her turn to be a prisoner," Rarazel added. "And I'm going to use my new freedom to help people with my plants. See how well Neptune's Fin grows already?"

"It looks like you and the plants are flourishing," Aquaman said. He pointed to a sleek, one-story structure in the center of the garden. "How do you like your new house?"

"I'm grateful it's not a tower!" Rarazel laughed. Then she rose up over the garden, stretched out her arms, and started to sing.

THE ORIGINAL STORY:
RAPUNZEL

Once upon a time, a couple was expecting a baby. The pregnant wife became hungry for a plant growing in a witch's garden nearby. The husband snuck in to steal it, but the witch caught him! As payment for the plant, she demanded the couple's baby. So when the day came, the witch took the child and named her Rapunzel.

Rapunzel grew up alone in a tall tower. The only way in was through a window near the top. The witch would call, "Rapunzel, Rapunzel, let down your hair!" Then the girl lowered her long locks out the window for the witch to climb.

One day, a prince was riding nearby and heard beautiful singing. He followed the song to the tower and saw the witch calling to Rapunzel. When the witch left, the prince called out in the same way. Down the hair came and up he climbed. At first, Rapunzel was afraid, but then the two talked. Soon, they were making plans for her to join the prince in his kingdom. The prince left with the promise to free Rapunzel.

Later, the witch came back. Rapunzel revealed she had seen the prince. The witch was furious! She cut off the girl's golden hair and sent her to a barren desert.

When the prince returned, the witch attacked him. He leaped from the tower and fell into a thorn bush. His eyes were badly scratched. He wandered blindly till he heard Rapunzel singing. The two were reunited, and Rapunzel's tears of joy healed the prince's eyes. They lived happily ever after.

SUPERPOWERED TWISTS

- The fairy tale starts with a husband trying to get a plant for his hungry, pregnant wife. This adventure begins with Aquaman searching for a powerful healing sea plant to help sick Atlanteans.

- The girl Rapunzel has long golden locks and lives in a tall, lonely tower. The mermaid Rarazel has living golden seaweed fronds and makes her home in an enchanted coral tower deep in the ocean.

- A prince hears singing and follows it to Rapunzel's tower. In this tale, Aquaman hears singing and vows to investigate. He isn't a prince, but he is the Sea King!

- Rapunzel is forced out of the tower by the angry witch. With the help of Aquaman and his finny friends, Rarazel escapes the tower's spell and gains her freedom.

- There's no marriage here, but Aquaman does take Rarazel to Atlantis where she lives happily ever after.

TALK ABOUT IT

1. Aquaman was suspicious of Gothal. Look back at the story and list at least three reasons why the hero thought the merwoman might be up to something.

2. When no one answered him, Aquaman decided to go into the coral tower. Do you agree with his choice? Why or why not?

3. Gothal had been lying to Rarazel for a long time. Think of a time when someone wasn't honest with you. How did you feel? Were you able to forgive that person?

WRITE ABOUT IT

1. How do you think Rarazel felt when Aquaman first climbed into her tower? Try rewriting the Chapter 2 scene from her point of view.

2. Create a file on Gothal for the Justice League's database. Write a description of the old sea witch's personality and powers.

3. Fairy tales are often told and retold over many generations, and the details can change depending on who tells them. Write your version of "Rapunzel." Change a lot or a little, but make it your own!

The Author

Laurie S. Sutton has been reading comics since she was a kid. She grew up to become an editor for Marvel, DC Comics, Starblaze, and Tekno Comics. She has written Adam Strange for DC, Star Trek: Voyager for Marvel, plus Star Trek: Deep Space Nine and Witch Hunter for Malibu Comics. There are long boxes of comics in her closet where there should be clothing and shoes. Laurie has lived all over the world and currently resides in Florida.

The Illustrators

Agnes Garbowska is an artist who has worked with many major book publishers, illustrating such brands as DC Super Hero Girls, Teen Titans Go!, My Little Pony, and Care Bears. She was born in Poland and came to Canada at a young age. Being an only child, she escaped into a world of books, cartoons, and comics. She currently lives in the United States and enjoys sharing her office with her two little dogs.

Sil Brys is a colorist and graphic designer. She has worked on many comics and children's books, having had fun coloring stories for Teen Titans Go!, Scooby-Doo, Tom & Jerry, Looney Tunes, DC Super Hero Girls, Care Bears, and more. She lives in a small village in Argentina, where her home is also her office. She loves to create there, surrounded by forests, mountains, and a lot of books.

GLOSSARY

betrayal (bih-TREY-uhl)—the act of being unfaithful and doing something that hurts a person who trusted you

cascade (kas-KEYD)—a large amount of something that flows down like a waterfall

down payment (DOWN PEY-muhnt)—the part of a price that is paid right when something is bought, with the rest due later

flourish (FLUR-ish)—to grow well; also, to be doing well

frond (FROND)—a leaflike part of seaweed

harvest (HAR-vist)—the picked plants from a crop; also, to pick plants

protect (proh-TEKT)—to keep safe from harm

summon (SUH-muhn)—to order or ask someone to come

telepathy (tuh-LEH-puh-thee)—the ability to communicate from one mind to another, without speech or signs

tendril (TEN-druhl)—a thin, twisting plant part

tentacle (TEN-tuh-kuhl)—a long, armlike body part some animals use to touch, grab, or smell

READ THEM ALL!